SHW

WHEEL WIZARDS

The #1 Sports Series for Kids

WHEEL WIZARDS

Little, Brown and Company

Boston   New York   London

To my great-grandson
Blake McKinley Howell

Copyright © 2000 by Catherine M. Christopher

First Edition

Matt Christopher™ is a trademark
of Catherine M. Christopher.

Library of Congress Cataloging-in-Publication Data

Hirschfeld, Robert.
    Wheel wizards / Robert Hirschfeld. — 1st ed.
        p.   cm.
    Summary: Angry and unhappy because he is now in a wheelchair
and apparently no longer able to play basketball, twelve-year-old Seth
is amazed to discover wheelchair basketball and finds that his life is
not over after all.
    ISBN 0-316-13611-5 (hc)/ISBN 0-316-13733-2 (pb)
    [1. Wheelchair basketball — Fiction.   2. Basketball — Fiction.
3. Wheelchairs — Fiction.   4. Physically handicapped — Fiction.
5. Sports for the physically handicapped — Fiction.]   I. Title.
PZ7.H59794 Wh   2000
[Fic] — dc21   00-030957

10 9 8 7 6 5 4 3 2 1

MV

Printed in the United States of America

I had the same dream last night," said Seth Pender. He smiled, thinking about it.

Seated in an armchair a few feet away, Brian Murtaugh nodded. "Want to tell me how the dream went?"

Seth's smile went out as if he'd flicked a switch, and he scowled instead. "What for?"

"I don't know . . . ," Brian replied. He was a tall man with reddish hair that he was always running his hands through. "How about just as a favor to me? Humor me, okay?"

With a sigh, Seth said, "It doesn't do any good, and, anyway, it's the same as all the other times. But all right. In the dream I'm playing basketball, and I'm really *hot.* I mean, I'm playing tough D, driving for layups, making twenty-foot jump shots, running down the court leading a fast break . . . everything. It's like I can't do anything wrong."

He smiled again but the smile faded quickly. "Then I wake up. End of dream."

Brian prodded. "You wake up, and . . . ?"

"What do you *think?*" Seth mumbled. "I see my legs, just lying there, like sticks. I remember the car accident, and I know I'll never play basketball again, or run again, or walk again. I know I'm trapped in this wheelchair for the rest of my life. End of the dream. End of all my dreams." Seth angrily slapped a hand on the arm of the chair and turned his face away to hide the tears that filled his eyes.

Seth was twelve years old. The accident that had cost him the use of his legs had happened several months earlier. Alarmed by his depression, Seth's parents had brought him to a therapist, in hopes that the man might help him deal with what had happened. Seth had been seeing Brian ever since.

But Seth's attitude hadn't changed yet. He was often sullen and angry, and he didn't like to talk to people much, even his family.

"So, you think your life is over?" Brian leaned forward in his chair, looking seriously at Seth.

Seth looked disgusted. "No, I 'don't think my life is over,'" he sneered. "Only the *good* part."

Brian sighed. "Seth, I know you find this hard to believe right now, but you have to have patience. Your mind needs time to heal, and once it does, you'll see that your life can be full and happy. In time —"

Seth's laugh had no humor in it. "Yeah, right. 'In time' I'll be just fine." He looked up at the therapist, hands clenched tight on the arms of his chair. "It's easy for *you* to talk. You don't get it. Nobody gets it. Why don't you just leave me alone? Why doesn't everyone *leave me alone?*"

"How did it go with Brian, today?" asked Mrs. Pender as she drove her son home from the therapist's office.

Slumped in the passenger seat, Seth muttered, "Same as always. 'I need to be patient. Someday everything will be wonderful again.' Blah, blah, blah."

He refused to say anything more until they got home. Mrs. Pender unfolded Seth's chair and offered to help him out of the car. Seth shook off her hand, hoisted himself into the chair, and wheeled himself inside. Once in the house, he headed straight for his room, slamming the door behind him.

He sat there for a moment, breathing hard, feeling angry and sick and unhappy, trying not to cry. He looked around, noticing the posters of his favorite basketball stars, which were scattered on the walls. Suddenly, they seemed to be a bad joke. It was as if they were saying, "See us, Seth? You'll *never* be able to do what we're doing!"

In a rage, he started ripping them down. Once he'd pulled down all that he could reach, he pushed himself out of the chair and onto his bed. He lay there, wishing that he could stay in bed forever and never have to face the world again. Nobody understood what he was going through, not his parents, not his friends, and certainly not that guy Brian, who kept saying that he needed patience, he had to give it time . . . *time* . . . Well, he had lots of that.

The time when he used to play sports, especially basketball. He closed his eyes and tried not to think at all.

There was a light knock on the door. He didn't say anything.

"Seth?" His mother's voice sounded timid. "Honey? Are you all right?"

"Oh yeah, I'm just fine," he said, not moving. "Leave me alone."

"Honey, Lou is here. Can he come in?"

Lou Aaron had been Seth's closest friend for years. But that was *before*.

Mrs. Pender opened the door. "Honey? Why not talk to Lou? He's been coming over every day, but you won't see him."

Seth stared at the ceiling. "Then he should take the hint and stay away."

"Hey, Seth!" Lou came into the room. "Listen, can we just talk a little? Aren't I still your friend? I was hoping you could come over tonight and we could watch some videos, maybe rent a movie —"

"Forget it." Seth refused to look at Lou. "Don't slam the door on your way out."

"Come on, Seth, the guys still want to be your friends. Give us a chance, huh?" Lou waited for an answer, but there was only silence from the bed.

"Well . . ." Lou shrugged. "Listen, if you want to come over, just give me a call. All right?"

Lou glanced at Mrs. Pender, shook his head, and slowly walked out of the room.

"Seth," she said, "I just wish you'd . . ." She stopped. "Dinner will be ready in half an hour. Is there anything you need?"

"Just close the door, Mom."

Sighing, Mrs. Pender closed the door.

At the dinner table, Mr. and Mrs. Pender looked at Seth's plate, where the food lay almost untouched. They exchanged a troubled look.

"Aren't you going to eat, son?" asked Mr. Pender. "Fried chicken is your favorite."

"And there's strawberry shortcake for dessert," Seth's mother added. When Seth neither spoke nor ate, she went on.

"You need to eat, honey. You'll make yourself sick if you don't —"

Seth laughed, but not happily. "Yeah, right, I don't want to ruin my health. Got to keep myself in tip-top shape."

Seth's sister, Phyllis, sixteen, slapped her fork down hard. "We know how rough this is for you, bro, but we're all on your side. We're trying to help.

Don't you get it? Why are you taking it out on us? It isn't our fault that you . . ."

She stopped, looking awkward.

Seth glared at her. "You 'know how rough this is'?" he mimicked. "*Sure* you do!" He laughed harshly. "Were you born dumb or did you get that way later?"

Mrs. Pender gasped. "*Seth!* Stop it!"

He ignored her. "And if I ask for your help, then okay. But I haven't asked, and I'm not asking. But still, you get in my face when I want to be left alone!"

Phyllis's face grew red. She got up quickly and almost ran from the room.

"*Seth!*" Mrs. Pender was furious. "Shame on you! We're your family, and you have no right to behave like this!"

"Is that right?" Seth wheeled himself away from the table. "I tell you what, why don't you ground me? That'll serve me right."

He turned away, but stopped and looked back at his parents. "I'll skip the strawberry shortcake, too."

He rolled out of the room.

2

After he had been really mean to his family, Seth always felt awful the next day. The following day was one of those days. That morning, he had wanted to apologize to everyone, but Phyllis and Mr. Pender had left very early, so he had only been able to speak to his mother.

"Sorry about last night, Mom," he had said. "I wish I could keep myself from doing that, but . . . I don't know . . . it just comes out and I can't stop it."

Mrs. Pender looked very tired, but she smiled and ran her hand through Seth's hair.

"I know," she said. "You're going through a very hard time right now. But we're sure that things won't stay this way, that you'll work it all out. Honey, we have to give it *time*. That's what Brian and your physical therapist say, and that's what we believe."

Seth shook his head. "I wish *I* could believe it. I mean, I guess I know that I won't always be as angry as I am, but . . . I just can't believe I'm ever going to be happy again."

Mrs. Pender kneeled in front of her son and put her hands over his on the chair arms. She looked into his eyes. "You *will*, dear. Dad and Phyllis and I — we all know it. You *will*."

"Mom, can we please not talk about it?"

His mother nodded and turned away. Seth knew she was crying, which made him feel even worse.

Later at school, Seth saw Lou in the hall and in a couple of classes. He thought about going over to speak to him, but he couldn't bring himself to do it — he didn't know what to say.

After classes, he headed toward the school library, where he figured he'd spend an hour doing homework. Mrs. Pender had arranged to pick him up afterward.

He was going down the corridor past the gym when he heard a familiar sound that made him stop. Someone was in there, dribbling and shooting a basketball. At first, Seth wasn't going to look, fearing that it would only depress him still more to see people doing what he no longer could. Then he decided that he couldn't feel worse than he did already, pushed open the doors, and stopped, amazed by what he saw.

In the middle of the basketball court, a guy dribbled a ball, stopped short, and took a fifteen-foot shot that went in off the glass. It was a good-looking shot.

And the shooter was in a wheelchair!

Seth stared in silence. The boy looked to be a few years older and had an awesome upper body, with a barrel chest and powerful arms. He picked up the ball and dribbled with one hand, using the other to wheel the chair incredibly fast toward the other end of the court. He stopped abruptly, pivoted the chair so he faced the basket, and took an even longer shot. This one dropped, too, barely moving the net.

Seth was astonished. How could the guy shoot like that sitting down? There was something weird about the chair, too. It looked like the wheels were loose, because they tilted in toward the top.

Seth noticed that the ball was rolling right at him. He reached for it but couldn't pick it up. Instead he used his fingertips to roll it back toward the other guy, who easily scooped it up one-handed.

"Thanks," the boy said, smiling.

"I watched you shoot. You're good!"

The older boy shrugged. "Thanks, I was in a groove there, I guess. My name's Danny Detweiler."

"Seth Pender." Seth started to wheel his chair onto the polished hardwood of the court.

"*Whoa!*" Danny held up a hand. "Don't bring that chair out here!"

Baffled, Seth stopped. "What's the problem?"

"You'll mark the floor up."

Seth pointed to Danny's chair. "Well, *you're* on the court, and I don't see any marks."

Danny nodded. "My chair is designed for sports, and it has special tires that won't leave skid marks on the wood. Your chair doesn't."

"Well, it looks like your special wheels are about to fall off. They're loose."

Danny grinned and shook his head. "They're meant to be like that. It's called 'camber,' and most sports chairs work that way, especially basketball chairs. The wheels are slanted on purpose."

"How come?" asked Seth. "For balance?"

"When you're playing a game, sometimes two chairs come together. Without the cambering, your hands could get mashed between the wheels."

Seth nodded, only half listening to the explanation. Something else Danny had said was just sinking in. "Did you say your chair is specially made for basketball?"

"Sure, wheelchair basketball. I've been playing a few years, and this year I'm starting league play. That's why I'm getting in as much gym time as I can. I need to work to be ready."

"Oh," said Seth. "*Wheelchair* basketball. I get you."

Danny's smile faded. "*What* do you get? What's with the look when you said 'wheelchair basketball'?"

Seth blinked. He had the feeling that Danny didn't like what he had said, but couldn't see why. "Well . . . I only meant . . . you know, *wheelchair* basketball. Not *real* basketball."

Now Seth was sure that Danny was angry. "Uh-huh," Danny said, giving Seth a flat stare. "*Real* basketball, like *you* used to play, I'll bet, before you wound up in that chair."

"Right," Seth replied. "I was good, too, but," he looked at the floor, "that's over for me, now."

"Yeah, that's a shame." Danny didn't sound sympathetic. In fact, he sounded sarcastic.

"Hey, you know what I mean," Seth said, worried

that he'd insulted Danny somehow. "I only got hurt a while ago, so I'm not . . . When did you have *your* accident?"

The older boy's eyes drilled into Seth's eyes. "I didn't have any accident. I had a birth defect; been using a wheelchair all my life."

Seth thought he understood. "Oh. Well, you're used to this, I guess. I mean, you *never* played *real* basketball. You don't know what I've been going through. It's like —"

"If you want a shoulder to cry on," Danny interrupted roughly, "you better look elsewhere. I'm busy." He started back onto the court, then turned back to face Seth.

"Actually, you sound like you're feeling sorry for yourself so you won't need any sympathy from me. By the way, I have a great life, and I happen to *love* wheelchair basketball. It's a great sport, but it's probably too much for you. See you around."

As he turned away, Seth left the gym, resentful over Danny's rudeness. *What's his problem?* he wondered. He'd hoped that Danny might turn out to be a new friend with whom he could share his troubles, but it didn't look like that would happen.

Outside the gym, a voice called, "Yo, Seth!"

It was Lou. Seth sighed. Earlier he had been looking for a way to apologize to his old friend. But after Danny's hostility, Seth didn't want company. Still, here came Lou anyway.

"Hey, Seth, some guys are coming over on Saturday to watch a game on TV, and I was thinking maybe you'd like to come, too."

"I don't think so," Seth replied, wanting the conversation to be over.

Lou frowned. "And that's that, huh? Listen, what's going on? You look like you want me to go away and stop bugging you. If you do, say the word and I'm gone."

Seth scowled. "That's what I've been trying to say for weeks."

"Fine," Lou said. "Now I understand. I won't bother you anymore. I guess you'd rather mope around than have friends. That's up to you. So long." Lou spun on his heel and stormed away.

Seth headed for the school door, his mind in turmoil. He wondered if he'd ever have another friend . . . or another really happy day.

3

The next morning, Seth was having breakfast with his family, and he told them about his encounter with Danny.

"Too bad he was such a creep. He looked really tough, and did he have a great outside shot! Anyway, he was going on about wheelchair basketball and how cool it was." Seth snorted. "Yeah, *right!*"

His sister took a bite of toast. "That reminds me, I heard something about a wheelchair-basketball league that is going to play some games here. My Phys. Ed. teacher, Ms. Fabini, mentioned it. She says there are women's *and* men's teams and that it's fun to watch. You should check it out, Seth. It might be something for you to try."

Seth shot a scornful look at Phyllis. "I don't *think* so."

15

"Why not?" asked Mr. Pender. "It sounds like a good idea to me."

"Come on, Dad! Are you kidding?" Seth waved a hand in disgust. "I played *real* basketball! And I was good! This wheelchair stuff has got to be totally lame."

"How do you know?" Phyllis demanded. "You've never played it. You've never *seen* it. Come on, bro, it's worth a look, anyway."

Seth stared straight ahead. "*You* look at it, if you want. I've got other things to do."

"Oh, really?" Phyllis leaned forward. "Like what, exactly? Like lying on your bed and sulking?"

Mrs. Pender put a hand on Phyllis's arm. "Honey, don't —"

Phyllis shook the hand off. "No, Mom, I'm sorry, but we've all been tiptoeing around because we're afraid of hurting Seth's feelings, which is more than I can say of *him.* But maybe we need to all say what's on our minds, because this other stuff isn't working.

"I *know* Seth loves sports and that he misses them a lot. And now we hear about something that he could actually play, and he just sits there and puts it down without even knowing anything about it. That's crazy to me."

Seth wheeled away from the table. "Everyone around here thinks they know what's best for me, but —"

"I don't say I know what's best for you," Phyllis interrupted, grabbing hold of his chair so he couldn't leave. "But I don't think *you* know what's best for you, either. Not the way you've been lately. Being rude and nasty to us when all we do is try to help. Turning your friends into enemies. Moping around like your life is over —"

"It *is* over!" Seth shouted. "Half of me doesn't work anymore and it never will again!"

Phyllis grabbed her brother's hand. "Your *brain* still works, if you'll let it! People can have wonderful lives even when they have a disability! You just won't let it happen, and it's . . . Let us help you, please! And start helping yourself, too." She let go of his hand and his chair to pound her fists against her knees in frustration.

Seth hung his head, staring silently at the floor. Deep down, he knew that Phyllis was right, but didn't have a clue about what to do or say, or how to begin to make something good out of his life.

He decided to start out small. That afternoon at school, he caught Lou's eye. Lou started to walk away, head down, but Seth called after him.

"Lou, wait a second!"

The other boy stopped and waited. His face was expressionless. "What do you want?"

Seth licked his lips, suddenly not sure of what he wanted to say. "Listen, if you never want to talk to me or have anything to do with me, after the way I've been acting lately, well, that's the way it has to be. I know I've been a total creep."

A small smile flickered over Lou's mouth. "Maybe not *total,* but pretty near."

"Well, I'm sorry," Seth said. "You've always been a good friend, and I know you still want to be. . . ."

"You got *that* right," Lou replied. "But you sure make it hard."

"I know," Seth mumbled, feeling miserable. Suddenly, the words just started pouring out of him. "I don't even know why I'm acting like this. I should feel so lucky to have friends like you and a family that wants to help, but I look at myself, and I feel like I'm trapped in this chair forever, and I get so *down.* And I say bad things, and I know I'm hurting people, but I can't stop myself."

Seth sighed. "The thing is, I still want to be friends. I'll try to act more like it from now on. I don't know for sure if it'll work, but I promise I'll try to treat you like a friend. If it's not too late, that is."

Lou studied Seth for a moment. "It's not too late. Let's take it from here and see how it goes, all right?" He stretched out a hand, and Seth grabbed it, hard. "All *right!*" Seth said.

Lou looked past Seth, and said, "There's Phyllis. She's headed this way, like she wants to talk to you."

Seth groaned and closed his eyes. "She probably wants to yell at me about this morning. I was acting like a jerk at breakfast."

Lou's eyes popped open in a cartoonish look of amazement. "*You?* Impossible!"

"I thought I saw you," said Seth's sister as she came up to them.

"Listen, Phyl," Seth began, "about this morning —"

Phyllis held up a hand. "I know. I guess I shot my mouth off way too much."

Seth shook his head. "No, you were right. It was me who —"

"Okay," Phyllis cut in again. "We've apologized to each other. Now come on. There's a poster I want you to see. Follow me."

As the boys went with Phyllis, Lou and Seth exchanged a look, and Seth shrugged. They stopped in front of a bulletin board by the gym door.

"What do you think?" Phyllis asked.

The poster read:

Game Sunday Night!!!
The Junior Wheelchair-Basketball League presents
The Rollin' Rebels vs.
The Wheel Wizards
Sunday, 8:00 PM

"Ta-da!" sang Phyllis. "Just like we were talking about! I think you should go."

"Hey, yeah," Lou agreed. "It sounds cool. What do you say, Seth?"

Seth made a face. "I don't know. Maybe another time."

Phyllis put her fists on her hips and stared at her

20

brother. "Another time? You have big plans for Sunday night?"

Seth shook his head. "No, but . . ."

"Come on, let's go," Lou urged. "I want to see what it's like. If it's dumb, we'll leave."

Seth raised his hands in a gesture of surrender. "Okay, all right. But don't blame me if you're bored out of your gourd."

Phyllis beamed at Lou as she took off. Lou cocked his head. "Sounds like someone's playing hoops right now." He opened the door a crack. "It's a guy shooting from a wheelchair!"

Seth looked past Lou. "It's this guy I met yesterday. His name is Danny, and I don't think he likes me much."

Suddenly Danny looked their way. He saw Seth and nodded in recognition. "How are you doing?"

"Okay," Seth said. "Can we come in?"

Danny smiled. "It's your gym."

Once inside, Seth introduced Danny and Lou to each other.

"You know anything about this game Sunday night?" asked Lou.

Danny bounced the basketball. "Sure. I'll be

playing. I'm with the Wheel Wizards, and it's the first game of the season."

"Hey, cool," Lou said. "We're going to the game, right, Seth?"

Danny looked at Seth. "That so? You coming? I hope you don't get bored, seeing that you used to play *real* basketball and all."

Seth felt his face turn red. "Uh, I'm sorry about what I said yesterday. I was dumb."

"Forget it," Danny replied. "Listen, the rest of the team is due soon for practice, so I can't talk now. But come early Sunday and watch the warmups and meet the rest of the team. I bet you change your mind about this game. It's pretty awesome."

"Cool!" Lou said.

"Sure, that'd be great," Seth agreed. They left the gym and headed out of the school.

It was a warm day and Seth wheeled himself home, with Lou walking beside him.

"I don't know why you thought Danny doesn't like you," Lou said after a while. "He seems to get along with you all right. And he's a nice guy, I think."

Seth laughed. "Yeah, he is. It was my fault. I

basically said that I thought wheelchair basketball wasn't real basketball, and he didn't like that at all."

Lou nodded. "I guess he wouldn't. Hey, he looks like a strong guy. Maybe this game is going to be better than you think."

"I doubt it," said Seth. "I mean, here's the thing: Danny has been in a wheelchair all his life, and it figures he'd think wheelchair basketball is neat. But I used to play *real* basketball."

"Maybe you shouldn't call it *real* basketball," Lou suggested. "I mean, there must be a way to put it that isn't so . . . well, insulting to a guy like Danny. And by the way, Danny looks to me like someone who feels good about his life, even if he's in a wheelchair. You might want to think about that."

Seth frowned. "Maybe. But I still think that it's different when someone has never been able to walk or run. It's less of a problem."

Lou replied, "And *I* still think your life will get a lot better, sooner than you think."

"You could be right," Seth said.

But he didn't think so.

4

On Sunday evening, Seth and Lou got to the gym an hour before the game was due to start. Nobody was there yet, except for a bunch of guys who were clearly players. Seth spotted Danny on the court at one free-throw line, practicing free throws, while several teammates tossed up shots from all around the basket. There was a similar grouping of players at the other end of the floor.

Lou pointed to Danny, saying, "Nobody's wearing uniforms yet, but I think these must be the Wheel Wizards, and those guys have to be the Rollin' Rebels."

Seth nodded, looking around curiously. In addition to the boys who were practicing shots, several others were scattered around the sidelines, doing things with their chairs. One boy sitting on a bench

24

appeared to be putting on a wheel; another sat in a wheelchair like Seth's and was adjusting some kind of cushion on another chair with cambered wheels. Lou nudged Seth and gestured to one of the Rollin' Rebels who had a bumper sticker on the back of his chair that said *Eat My Dust*.

When the guy with the bumper sticker turned their way, Seth saw that he had a burly upper body, but that his legs only extended to his knees. Seth became aware that the athletes on the court had a wide range of disabilities. Some had only one leg, some had no legs at all. He was startled to see one player get out of his wheelchair, stand up, and walk slowly toward the sidelines to get a towel. He had heavy braces on both knees.

A few minutes later, Danny saw Seth and Lou, waved to them, and came over.

"You made it," he said, shaking hands with both boys. "Good to see you."

"There are some awesomely muscular dudes out there," Lou observed.

Danny nodded. "You got *that* right. When you use your arms and upper body like we do, even if you *don't* work out, you get pretty buffed." He looked at

Seth. "I bet your upper body is stronger than it used to be. Am I right?"

Seth thought for a moment and realized it was true. "Yeah," he admitted. "I can do things now, like getting in and out of a car, pretty easily. It used to be a major effort." The more he thought about it, the more he realized it was true.

"Anyway," Danny said, "I want you to meet the other Wizards."

"That'll be neat," Seth replied. "Hey, there are players who can walk."

"Sure," said Danny. "If this was the adult division of the league, we'd get ratings according to how disabled we are. A guy who can walk is in what they call Class III, and his rating is three points. If you're like Warren over there," he continued, pointing to a player with no legs, "you're Class I and have a rating of one point. No team can have a total of more than twelve rating points on the floor at a time. It keeps things evenly matched. But in the junior division we're not rated."

Danny waved to the guy who had walked over for a towel. "Yo, Gary! Come and meet my buddies." Gary wheeled his chair over. He had on a sweatshirt

26

that was cut off at the shoulders. While he was leaner than Danny, the muscles of his arms were impressive.

"Guys, this is Gary Vitaglio," said Danny, before introducing Seth and Lou.

Gary shook hands, smiling. He studied Seth for a moment. "How long have you been in that chair?"

"Five months," Seth replied.

Gary nodded. "I know it's rough, at first. I got hurt when I was eight, and I thought, *That's it, my life is over.* But, Seth, I'm telling you, I was wrong. You'll see. You can have a really good life. It's all a matter of attitude. Ask anybody here." He turned to another teammate who had come over to join them. "Right, Con? Seth and Lou, this is Con Addams. He can shoot the lights out when he's hot . . . which is, like, once a month or so."

Con grinned. "Look who's talking. If we had a rating system, Gary would get a minus three, and we could put two extra men on the court."

Con was square-faced and blond. A sweatband kept his hair out of his eyes. Seth found himself staring at Con's shrunken legs, and he blushed.

Con noticed. "That's the way they've been all my life, so *I'm* used to them. They tell me it was a birth defect. But, hey, we all have our problems, right, Gary?"

Gary and Con exchanged a low five. Gary said, "Con has big plans — he's going to be a star in two sports."

"Right," Con said. "I'm going to play basketball right through college and compete in the Paralympics some day. *And* I'm going to do marathons, too. Boston, New York, the biggies."

"The Paralympics?" Lou asked.

"It's like the Olympics for disabled athletes. There are competitions in lots of events, for men and women. It's the big time for wheelchair sports."

Seth was impressed. He pointed to Con's chair. "That looks pretty hot."

Con patted the chair arm. "The frame is made of a superlight alloy, like they use for racing-bike frames, and I just put on these incredible wheels." He pointed to the other end of the court. "I'm going to make those Rebels sweat tonight. They better be *ready*."

A shrill whistle rang out. "Uh-oh, it's that time," Danny said. "See you later, Seth, Lou."

"Nice meeting you," added Gary.

"Enjoy the game," Con said.

The three Wizards joined their teammates in a circle around their coach, a man in a wheelchair wearing a warmup suit.

Lou sat in the bottom row of the bleachers with Seth next to him as both teams began their regular pregame drills.

They started with a layup drill much like Seth was used to. The players formed two lines. The first in one line moved in for a layup, dribbling if necessary. The leader of the second line raced forward to either get the rebound or pick up the ball after the made basket and fed an assist to the next player in line number one, and so forth. Seth and Lou had seen and done it many times.

Except, these guys were doing it in wheelchairs, maneuvering the chairs and handling the ball with incredible skill. Most of the shots were made.

For a few minutes, both boys watched without saying a word. Finally, Lou spoke. *"Amazing!"*

Seth nodded. He had to admit it was impressive. The coach's whistle ended layups, and the players began a shootaround, taking one- and two-handed shots, as well as hook shots, from various distances. Seth watched openmouthed as Gary Vitaglio raced his chair toward midcourt at astonishing speed, leaning forward, hands pumping the wheels, and then used the heel of one hand to brake one wheel, stopping the chair's forward motion and pivoting sharply.

Lou nudged Seth with an elbow. "See that guy with the blue shirt? He just made his fourth straight eighteen-footer! Just with arms and upper body! I'm not believing some of this!"

Seth was surprised to realize that he was looking forward to the game itself. He had expected the whole evening to be boring, depressing, or both.

Con Addams came over to them. "How are you doing?"

"Fine," replied Seth. "This is awesome! I can't believe the shooting, and the way you can move, the speed and how you stop and spin. It's amazing!"

Con grinned. "You have any questions?"

"Are the rules any different?" From *real* . . . uh, I mean . . ."

"We call it 'full-bodied' basketball," Con interrupted. "And the rules are basically the same: two points for most baskets, except three points for shots from behind the three-point line, a point for free throws, same fouls, same size court, same basket height, same basketball. Oh yeah, there's a thirty-five-second shot clock. If you don't get a shot up that hits at least the rim or the backboard within thirty-five seconds of getting possession, that's a turnover." He scratched his head, thinking.

"There are a few things about height regulations for chair seats, the kinds of cushions you can use, stuff like that, but mostly it's the same game."

Seth saw that some other people were coming into the gym, including a group who carried a banner that read *Wizard Power!!!*

Con saw them and waved. He gestured to the group with a thumb and explained, "That's our official rooting section. Friends and family who come to just about all the games."

"How long are the games?" asked Seth.

"We play eight-minute quarters. The adults and college teams play twenty-minute halves. Just like . . . ," he stopped and grinned. "Just like *real* ball."

Con was about to go on when the coach called to him. He shrugged.

"Time to suit up and go over the game plan. See you later. Have fun!"

The two teams disappeared into the locker rooms as more people filed into the gym and sat in the bleachers around Seth and Lou. Seth saw two girls unfold another banner. This one read *Rebels Rule!*

"What do you think?" Lou asked.

"Ask me after the game is over," Seth answered. He didn't want to admit yet that maybe he might have been wrong about wheelchair basketball.

Among the spectators, he noted that there were a number in wheelchairs, seated, as he was, in front of the stands. There were also plenty of able-bodied fans, too.

When the teams emerged on the court a few minutes later there were cheers, and fans called out encouragement. The Wizards' jerseys were black and gold, while the Rebels' colors were red and blue. The teams huddled around their coaches, who both used wheelchairs.

The Wizard coach seemed to be giving his group a pep talk and reminding them about the game plan. When he finished, the players leaned forward and joined hands.

The coach said something Seth couldn't catch, and the Wizards barked out, *"Teamwork!"* Five players moved out onto the court, leaving the six others on the sideline.

At the other end, the Rebels shouted, *"Play tough!"* Their starters came on. One of the two refs tossed a coin. The Wizard captain called, "Heads," and won the toss, meaning that the Wizards would put the ball inbounds to begin the game.

At the moment a Wizard inbounded the ball — a bounce pass to Danny — Gary sped downcourt as hard as he could, head forward, sinewy arms working like pistons. Two Rebels shot off in pursuit, but the Wizards had caught them off guard. Danny fired a baseball pass. Gary looked back just in time to see the ball, grabbed it, dribbled once, and laid it in for two points.

The Wizard fans cheered, waving their banner, and Seth found that he was cheering, too. He and Lou exchanged grins.

The Rebels moved the ball upcourt more deliberately, while one muscular, heavyset boy moved into the paint under the Wizard basket. Lou leaned over to Seth and said, "It must be hard to force a guy that big outside."

Seth nodded. "Yeah, looks like size and strength

make a huge difference in wheelchair hoops, just like in regular basketball."

As the Rebels advanced, making use of several passes, the Wizard coach yelled out, "Where's the ball? *Watch the ball!*"

Sure enough, as Seth and Lou had expected, the Rebels got the ball to the big guy in the middle, and three Wizards converged on him. But, instead of shooting, the guy passed to another Rebel directly behind him. Then he raised his arms, creating a huge obstacle. Con tried desperately to get around him to block the shot.

Lou whistled. "Great pick! He's like a wall out there in the paint."

The Rebel shot rolled off the rim. But the player who had set the pick grabbed the ball and passed to a teammate, who tried to move toward the basket along the baseline. Con moved in to block him and the chairs collided.

A ref's whistle stopped play.

"That's a charge," Lou guessed.

But Seth shook his head. "I think Con was still moving. It's on him."

Sure enough, the ref pointed to Con. "That's blocking on black, number eight."

Con winced but said nothing, and the Rebels inbounded the ball.

As the game went on, Seth found himself getting more and more involved, cheering whenever the other Wizard rooters cheered, exchanging high fives with Lou when his team (as he now thought of them) scored or made a good defensive play. He was fascinated by the way in which the players set picks, screened off, went from man-to-man defense to zones, and, in general, played the same kind of basketball he knew and loved.

At halftime, Lou asked, "You bored?"

"*Bored?*" Seth laughed. "Are you kidding? This is great." He thought for a moment. "Uh, I guess I was wrong about this game, wasn't I?"

Lou smiled. "I guess so. How about finding out how you can start playing yourself?"

"Absolutely!" Seth felt more excited, more alive, than he had in a long time. "Right after the game, I'm going to talk to Danny and those guys about what I should do."

During the second half, the lead moved back and forth, never going above four points. Both coaches substituted freely, and every player got in some time. Danny scored two baskets, but his main role was setting up plays and passing. Gary seemed to be the fastest of the Wizards, while Con played stubborn defense and forced some turnovers. The Wizards finally went ahead to stay and won the game, 39–36.

After members of the teams had shaken hands and fans were talking to the players, Danny and Gary came up to Seth and Lou, who congratulated them.

Seth was so excited, he couldn't find words. "This was . . . You guys are . . ."

Danny and Gary grinned at each other. "Guess you liked it, huh?" Danny said.

"*Liked* it?" Seth wheeled closer to the two Wizards. "I want to play! Is there any way I could get on your team?"

Danny raised his hands. "Whoa! Take it easy. There's no way you're ready yet."

"But —"

"First of all, you're not old enough to play on a team like this," said Gary. "And you're not in shape."

Seth felt terrible, and it showed in his face. Danny noticed.

"Don't get us wrong. You *can* play this game, someday. But you're going to have to get yourself ready. You need to train for it. Don't think it'll be easy, either. It's a tough road. But you can do it, if you want to."

Gary nodded agreement. "Like I said before, it's all in the attitude. Set yourself a goal, get your head in the right place, and it'll happen." He glanced at Danny. "We'd better get to the locker room."

Danny shook hands with Seth and Lou. "Listen," he said, "I'll be in touch."

Seth watched them go, feeling let down. Lou looked curiously at his friend. "What's the matter? I thought you'd be pumped about tonight."

"I was," Seth said, "until they blew me off like they did."

"Oh, come on! They didn't do that at all! They just said you have to get ready. And you *can.* If it's worth it to you."

"Are you kidding? *Sure* it's worth it!"

Lou smiled. "Then do it! You're the *man!*"

5

Brian Murtaugh leaned back in his chair and studied Seth. "Well, how's it going?"

"Pretty good, I guess," Seth replied. "Why are you looking at me like that?"

"Why?" Brian smiled. "I just asked you how it's going and you said, 'Pretty good.'"

"Yeah. So?"

"So, that's the first time since you started coming here that you've had anything positive to say. You took me by surprise."

"Really?" It was Seth's turn to be surprised. "The *first time?*"

Brian nodded. "I think I'll mark it in red on my calendar. So, naturally, I want to know how come you feel pretty good."

Seth thought for a moment. "I don't know. I just . . . feel better today, that's all."

"Uh-huh." Brian ran a hand through his hair. "You just woke up this morning and decided you felt better? That's it?"

"Well," Seth said, grinning, "there *was* something else."

Brian snapped his fingers. "A-*hah!* I had a hunch there was something else. What was the something else?"

"I went to this wheelchair-basketball game, and it was really neat. And I met these guys who play wheelchair basketball."

"Tell me more," urged the therapist.

Seth told Brian about Danny Detweiler, Gary Vitaglio, and Con Addams. He described the game between the Wheel Wizards and the Rollin' Rebels, how impressive the players had been, how he had enjoyed the game.

"I've seen some games," Brian said. "You're right about how good those athletes are. You ought to take a look at the people who compete in marathon races in wheelchairs — men and women, both. They're amazing, too."

"Yeah, that guy Con says he's going to do marathons someday, and play college hoops, and compete in these Olympics for disabled people. . . ."

"The Paralympics," offered Brian.

"Yeah, that's it," Seth nodded eagerly. "Anyway, I guess seeing those guys and what they can do made me feel pretty good, too."

"That's understandable," Brian agreed. "So, now, do you want to get involved in wheelchair athletics, yourself?"

Seth's grin faded and he slumped a little in his chair. "After the game, I asked Danny and the other guys if I could play, but . . ."

He trailed off, staring at the floor.

"But . . . ? prompted Brian.

"They said I couldn't"

Brian frowned. "You *couldn't?* Meaning what? That you weren't allowed? That they didn't want you to play? Is that what they meant, do you think?"

Seth said nothing for a long moment, considering Brian's question. "Well, no, that's not what they *said.* Not actually."

Brian's question was soft. "What did they say . . . *actually?* You remember?"

Seth closed his eyes, concentrating. "They said I wasn't old enough, that I wasn't in shape, stuff like that."

"Um-hum. But you took that to mean that they didn't want you to play, at least not with them?"

"Well . . . yeah." Seth scowled.

Brian crossed his legs and sat back. "How old are Danny and the others?"

"Fifteen, I think."

"Fifteen." Brian shrugged. "If you weren't in that wheelchair and you watched some fifteen-year-old boys playing able-bodied ball, would you walk up and ask if you could play in their league?"

Seth chewed on his lower lip. "Um, no, I guess not."

Brian went on. "From what you said, these guys are all in fantastic shape, right?"

Seth nodded. "Yeah, they're totally buffed."

"Would you say that *you're* in that kind of shape right now?" asked Brian.

Seth felt his face redden, and he looked away from Brian. "Uhn-uhn. No way." He looked up and met the therapist's eyes. "I think I see what you're saying."

"What am I saying?"

"You're saying that when Danny said I was too young and I'm not in shape, he just meant that I'm too young and not in shape. Not that he didn't want me to play."

Brian snapped his fingers. "You know, I think you may have something, there! Maybe they weren't putting you down, but just trying to tell you the truth."

Smiling, Seth replied, "Yeah, I guess."

"Now that you're on a hot streak, I have another question for you to think about. Ready?"

"Sure," Seth replied warily.

"Okay." Brian leaned forward again, looking steadily at Seth. "Why do you think you believed that Danny and Gary and Con were putting you down, when they were only trying to explain something to you?"

"I don't know," Seth said, without pausing.

Brian raised his eyebrows. "You don't know? Really? You *sure* you don't know?"

Seth felt himself getting irritated. "How should I know what those guys were thinking? I'm not a mind-reader!"

Brian waved Seth's words away with a hand. "I'm

not asking you to read *their* minds. I'm asking you to read *yours.*"

"That's pretty dumb!" Seth snapped. "What time is it, anyway? Isn't it time for this to be over?"

"Soon," Brian answered. "But not just yet. I think we should stay with this a little longer."

"Well, I *don't.*"

Brian remained cool. "Humph. Getting a little angry, there?"

Seth clenched his fists. "So what if I am?"

"So nothing," Brian said, still cool. "You get angry a lot, don't you?"

Seth rolled his eyes. "This is getting bo-o-o-ring."

"Humor me," urged Brian. "How did you feel when Danny said you couldn't play on his team?"

"I felt like he was putting me down! And it wasn't fair!" shouted Seth. "It isn't fair! Nothing's fair!"

Brian said nothing for a moment. Seth's words hung in the air.

"You're right, Seth," he said, at last. "A lot of things aren't fair. Your accident wasn't fair. Neither was what happened to Con or Gary or Danny. People should be fair to each other, but sometimes *life* isn't. And that can make someone really angry."

43

Seth nodded, feeling a little ashamed of having lost it.

Brian went on. "And the really awful thing about it is, when life treats you unfairly, what can you do about it? Who can you complain to? Who can you get mad at in return?"

The boy let out a deep breath. "Nobody," he whispered.

The therapist stood up, walked over to Seth, and put a hand on his shoulder. "Nobody who *deserves* it, anyway. Right. *But . . .*" he walked around to face Seth and squatted down so they were at eye level. "*But . . .* you still get *mad.* It's natural.

"So there you are, with all that *mad* boiling in your stomach, and what are you going to do with it?"

Seth blinked. He swallowed. "Get mad at somebody else?"

Brian nodded. "Bingo. Maybe at your friends. Or your family. Or even poor little me."

Seth felt suddenly as though a blindfold had been removed from his eyes. Then he shook his head.

"Okay, so I get mad a lot, and I take it out on other people. But what am I supposed to do? I mean, how am I going to stop?"

Brian sat back down. "What we hope is that there'll come a time when you don't get mad anymore. And you've just taken a big step in the right direction, by realizing what's been going on in your head for the last several months. Now, we can hope that you can see it coming and start to control that anger, so it doesn't hurt the wrong people.

"Another big step for you is finding out that you have a *future*. Setting yourself a goal — like playing wheelchair sports — means that you're likely to focus more on what you're capable of doing, and less on what happened and how rotten a break you got. And, Seth . . . you can do a *lot*."

Seth suddenly felt tired, but relaxed. "Yeah," he said. "Maybe. I see. *Yeah*."

"And now," Brian said as he got to his feet again, "our time really *is* up."

That night, before dinner, Seth thought long and hard about what he and Brian had talked about that day. He thought about Lou, and Phyllis, and his parents, and all they had been trying to say to him. He thought about Danny and Con and the others, too. And he made a decision.

That night during dinner, Seth asked, "Is it okay if I go to a movie with Lou and some guys on Friday?"

His father almost dropped his fork, but pretended he hadn't. "Sure," he replied as nonchalantly as he could.

"Oh, and one other thing," Seth added as he cut a bite off his roast beef and tried not to see the hopeful look on his mother's face. "I want to ask my physical therapist about what kind of exercise I should do to train for basketball."

"You going to play ball with those guys you watched the other night?" Phyllis asked.

"Maybe someday, but I'm not ready yet. I have to get in shape first. And, hey, Phyl? Thanks for telling me about that game."

"Hey, it wasn't any big deal," his sister replied.

Seth smiled at her. "Oh, yeah, it was. Trust me. It was a *very* big deal."

6

Seth sat in his brand-new wheelchair, feeling a little nervous. His parents had given him the chair on his thirteenth birthday, a week before. It felt strange, compared to his old chair, but it also felt *good*.

The old chair sat by the wall of the gym, where Seth and six other boys were about to begin their first workout as a basketball team.

Lou had been at Seth's house when Mr. and Mrs. Pender had wheeled out Seth's gift, and he had watched Seth sit in it for the first time.

"Looking *good!*" he'd exclaimed. "I'll bet you can really move in that baby!"

Seth looked up at his family, amazed and speechless. He hadn't expected this, because sports chairs, with their superlight frames and custom details,

47

were expensive. He touched the cambered wheels and tried to think of the right words.

"This is . . . It's . . . *Thanks!* Mom, Dad, it's totally great! But, I never figured we could afford it. I mean a chair like this . . ."

"Where there's a will, there's a way," said his dad. "You really have your sister to thank. She did all the research into chairs." Seth shot his sister a huge grin. "Your mom and I just signed on the dotted line and hid the box. We wanted to show you how proud we are of you. You should feel proud of *yourself.*"

"With this new team starting," Phyllis added, "we figured you needed it now. I mean, you've been working hard this year, so we wanted to do our share."

"How does it feel?" Lou had asked as Seth tried moving it around.

Seth smiled happily. "It's *unreal.* It doesn't weigh anything at all!"

Phyl had been right; Seth had been working hard for the past months. With the help of his physical therapist, he'd started a weight-lifting program, learned to swim using just his arms, and found a place to do laps in his chair. Now, Seth felt primed for his first-ever wheelchair-basketball practice. He didn't know any of his teammates-to-be, who all looked to be his age, and who all were in chairs resembling his.

"Is that new?" asked a boy next to Seth, pointing at Seth's wheelchair. "It looks cool."

Seth nodded. "Yeah, I just got it."

The other boy said, "I'm Pete Gould."

"Seth Pender."

"You ever play basketball?" asked Pete.

Seth shook his head. "Not in a chair, anyway. I've been watching games, though."

"Yeah, me too." Pete flexed his hands nervously. "Those guys are amazing."

"Really," Seth agreed. "I hope we —"

He stopped abruptly as the gym doors opened and three newcomers entered. All were in wheelchairs. One was a man with light-blond hair in a buzz cut.

The other two, Seth was happily surprised to see, were Danny Detweiler and Con Addams. Seth hadn't seen much of Danny or Con recently, since neither went to his school, and he grinned at them.

Danny and Con gave him nods of recognition, but didn't say a word. Seth felt slightly hurt.

The man clapped his hands sharply. "Form up over here, and let's get started."

The boys grouped themselves around him, and the man looked at each one in turn.

"My name is Wes van Valk, and I'm your coach. These two," he said, pointing to Danny and Con, "are my assistants. They play in the Junior Division. I've been playing this game since I was your age, played in college, and was on an NWBA team — that's National Wheelchair-Basketball Association, by the way.

"You can expect to work very hard over the next few weeks, before we get to play a game. Figure on feeling some aches and stiffness, especially at first. If that's a problem for you, then this isn't your sport. I don't know *what* your sport is, because I believe in the old saying 'No pain, no gain.' Understood?"

Seth and the others nodded that they did, although Pete Gould caught Seth's eye and made a face.

After the boys had introduced themselves to each

other and the coaches, the first practice session began. That whole day, Seth and the other boys never touched a ball. Wes had them working with their chairs, doing what he called "wind sprints," racing at top speed from baseline to baseline, learning how to bring themselves from high speed to a quick stop, and how to make their chairs pivot sharply. Seth had thought that he was in pretty good condition after having spent almost a year working out, but he found himself puffing and sweating before long.

After forty-five minutes, Con noticed Pete Gould shaking his hands and wincing.

"Is there a problem, Pete?" he asked.

"My hands feel like they're burning up," the boy answered. "Can't we wear gloves or something?"

Con shook his head. "No gloves. Give it a little time, your skin will toughen up. You have to develop calluses, that's all." He held up his own hands and smiled. "Like leather," he said. "Tough it out."

Pete sighed, and Seth, whose hands were bothering him, too, sympathized, but didn't say a word.

During a break, Pete came over to Seth. "Am I the only one here whose hands are bothering him? Tell me I'm not."

51

Seth laughed. "You're not, believe me. Mine are probably just as bad, and I see other guys looking like they're hurting, too. But, like the coach says —"

"'No pain, no gain,' right, I remember," Pete said. "I just hope the gain is worth the pain."

"Seth, how are you doing?" It was Danny, who had come up to the two boys as they talked.

"Good," Seth replied. He had wondered why Danny and Con hadn't been more friendly to him today, but had decided that he shouldn't fall into his old pattern and take it personally. There was probably a reason.

Danny looked Seth over a moment and gave him a nod of approval. "I can see you've been in training. It really shows in your arms. You feel the difference?"

Seth suddenly felt much better. "Yeah, it really feels good. When I started out, I used to get really wiped out in a few minutes. Now I can do so much more, with weights, exercises, it's great."

Danny lightly punched Seth's arm. "Wait till we've finished with you. You'll *really* be tough then, I guarantee you."

"When do we get to really play ball?" asked Pete.

"When you're ready," Danny answered. "Wes wants you to learn how to use your chairs — that's the first thing. Then you're going to work on the mechanics: dribbling, passing, and so on. It's not much fun, but it has to be done."

"So we won't even be doing any shooting today?" Seth asked, feeling let down.

"You want to do some shooting?" asked Wes, who had overheard Seth's question. "Get a ball, find a hoop, and shoot all you like. But what we have to do here, as a team, is make players of you. The fun part comes later."

He raised his voice so the others could hear. "Okay, we've had our rest. Time to get back to work."

Pete groaned, but softly, so only Seth could hear. He gave Seth a look of exaggerated fatigue that almost made Seth laugh out loud. But he held it in. He decided he liked Pete, and hoped he would stay with the team.

After practice ended, he asked Pete, "Want to hang out with some of my friends and me this weekend?"

Pete's face lit up in a smile. "I'll check with my

folks. But I think so, yeah. Thanks. If I've recovered by then."

Outside, while Seth waited to be taken home, Danny came up to him. "Listen, I do some shooting over at the elementary school playground on weekends. Maybe we can plan a time for you to join me?"

"Hey, sure. That'd be neat."

Seth felt flattered that Danny had invited him. And he had a feeling that, in Pete, he had a new friend. It had been an excellent day.

7

"You sure are in a bad mood today," Lou said as they walked to the gym, where Seth was due to practice. "What's the problem?"

Seth shrugged. It was a week after the first practice, and a hard week it had been, too. "Maybe it's nothing. But I think the coach is getting on my case way too much. It's getting to be a total drag."

"You mean, he's hassling you in particular?" asked Lou. "Or that he just rides everybody too hard?"

"Not everybody, just *me*," Seth snapped. "I don't get it. I work as hard as all the other guys, and I think I may be better than most of them. But it's like I can't do anything right, and whatever I do, he puts me down."

Lou walked a few paces before he said, "Did you ask him about it?"

"Yeah! Of course I asked him about it! I'm not stupid!"

Lou raised a hand. "Okay, okay, lighten up! I'm just asking."

"Sorry," Seth said. "I asked the coach if there was something I was doing wrong, or had said that bothered him, and he said that if I did something wrong, I'd hear about it. Pete noticed it, too. He asked what I'd done to get the coach mad at me."

"Maybe you can talk to Danny," Lou suggested.

But Seth shook his head. "Bad idea. I thought about it, but I don't think Danny would be happy. I mean, he's my friend, but he's also the coach's assistant, and he doesn't want to be put in the middle."

As they reached the gym door, Lou said, "Well, maybe it'll just blow over. Anyway, I hope so. See you."

Seth waved to his friend, took a deep breath, and entered the gym. The rest of the players and the coaches were already there.

"Where were you?" Wes demanded, looking at his watch.

Seth stared at him. "I thought practice started at four o'clock. It's not even four yet."

"Guess a star athlete like you doesn't have to bother warming up," said the coach. "When I say that practice starts at four, I mean be ready to go to work at four. I *don't* mean show up at four."

Seth clenched his jaws tight and tried not to let his anger show. After a moment, he said, "Sorry. It won't happen again."

Wes nodded and turned to face the other boys. "We're going to work on our dribbling today. Form two lines for a relay race."

Seth suppressed a groan and tried not to let his nervousness show. Although he was making good progress in other parts of the game, he was still having trouble with dribbling, especially coordinating it with keeping his chair moving where he wanted it to go. It seemed that he was always either losing the ball or letting the chair go off to the side, or both.

And now they were doing this relay race, in which two lines of players were competing teams. A player from each team dribbled from one end of the court to the other and then passed the ball to the next teammate, until all four players had gone. As he got on the end of one line, Seth was dreading messing up and causing his team to lose.

Pete, who was the anchorman on the other team, noticed the expression on his friend's face and leaned toward him. "Just be cool," he whispered. "You can do it."

Seth smiled weakly.

The race was close, and as Seth and Pete set themselves in their chairs, Seth's team had a slight lead. He got the ball and started downcourt as fast as he could. Out of the corner of his eye he could see Pete just behind him.

Seth knew that he should be able to dribble without watching the ball so he could keep an eye on where he was going, but he couldn't stop himself from shifting his eyes to his dribbling. As he did, his chair swung into Pete's path.

"Pender, watch where you're going!" shouted the coach. Startled, Seth tried to get back into his lane. As he did so the ball hit his wheel and caromed away. Disgusted, he stopped and stared at it.

Wes's voice was like a whiplash. *"Get the ball, Pender!* You going to sleep out there?"

Feeling angry and embarrassed, Seth raced after the ball, grabbed it, and headed back to finish his leg of the relay. He noticed that Pete had stopped and was waiting for him.

"*Gould!*" the coach yelled. "You're in a race, remember? Get moving!"

Pete quickly finished the race, leaving Seth trailing by several seconds. Seth wished that he could find a hole to hide in. Why was the coach being so unfair?

Wes wheeled up to Seth and grabbed the ball. "Maybe you should think about getting here early and working on your dribbling. You sure need the work."

Seth felt the eyes of all the other players on him and felt his jaws clench. The coach looked at him for a moment and turned away.

"Let's move on, people. We have a lot to do this afternoon."

The practice went on, with Wes riding Seth despite the fact that Seth was improving quickly. At one point, as the coach was having the team work on a new defense against a pick, Seth and a teammate slammed together. Off balance, Seth tumbled out of his chair onto the hardwood floor. Pete and two others rushed to help him up, but Wes stopped them with a blast of the whistle.

"Let him alone. Seth can get up by himself," he said. Pete gave the coach a look of surprise, but Seth said, "I'm okay."

Setting his wheel brakes, he hoisted himself back into his seat. The coach nodded. "You all need to be as independent as possible. One way to get there is not to look for help when you can do something by yourself. That doesn't just apply to basketball, by the way."

A few minutes later, Pete edged over to Seth. "You all right?" he asked.

Seth shrugged. "I'm not hurt, if that's what you mean. Yeah, I guess I'm all right."

Pete shook his head. "I was going to help you up, but —"

"But he didn't need your help." Con Addams had heard Pete and was staring hard at him and Seth. "Coach is right. The more you can do for yourself, the better off you are, and you'd better understand what that means."

Seth stared back at Con. "I didn't ask anyone to help me up, did I? I did it myself."

Con nodded, unsmiling, and the team resumed practice. They worked on passing and a few offensive plays. Wes seldom praised anyone and got on some players for not paying attention or taking it too easy. Seth did neither, but still got criticized. By the end of practice, he had had all he could stand and headed quickly for the exit, not speaking to anyone.

He heard someone calling his name as he rolled toward the parking lot, but didn't stop until he was outside. As he sat there, taking deep breaths and trying to relax, Danny came up alongside him.

"You okay?" he asked.

Seth snorted. "Oh, I'm just great."

"If you have something on your mind, maybe you should spit it out," suggested Danny.

Seth wheeled around to face the other boy. "I'm tired of being picked on all the time! It's not fair! I'm doing as well as I can, and I think I'm picking everything up just fine. Well, maybe not the dribbling. But no matter what I do, he finds something to get on my back about. What does the coach have against me, anyway? Do *you* know?"

Danny sighed. "He doesn't have anything against you. I think he feels you're doing a good job."

61

"He sure has a funny way of showing it! He's never said one nice thing to me."

"Have you heard the coach say anything nice to *anybody*?" asked Danny.

Seth thought for a moment. "Well . . . no. But he's still got it in for me, and I don't know how much more I can take. If he keeps doing it, I think I may quit!"

Danny studied Seth for a long, silent minute. Finally, he spoke.

"I think it'd be a real shame if you quit the team, Seth. But, you know what? That's your decision to make. See you tomorrow."

Danny turned and moved away, leaving Seth staring after him.

Maybe I'll just quit the team."

Seth was on his way to a session with Brian, and Lou was walking with him.

"You really think you want to do that?" asked Lou, frowning. "Don't you think that would be going too far? I mean, you've been looking forward to this, working out . . ."

They stopped to wait for a traffic light. "I *was* looking forward to it," Seth agreed, "but I never figured on being picked on all the time."

As they crossed the street, Lou asked, "Did you tell Danny? What does he think?"

"He said it was up to me, but I think he's on Coach's side. Con, too."

"Really? Huhn."

Seth turned and stared at his friend. "What does 'huhn' mean?"

"Well . . ." Lou chewed on his lower lip. "I don't know your coach, but Danny and Con are cool guys."

"I think so, too," Seth admitted. "Or I *did*, anyway. Now, I don't know. So you think they're all right and I'm all wrong, is that it?"

Lou raised his hands and smiled at Seth. "Hey, I'm your friend, remember. I'm on your side. It's just that . . . I think it'd be too bad if you quit. You could be really good at this, and getting yourself ready for it has done great things for you.

"I mean, *look* at you! You're in really good shape, and you've been so much more upbeat since this game came into your life. I hope you'll think twice before you do anything final, that's all."

They had arrived at Brian's office. Seth took a deep breath and grinned at Lou. "I know you're my friend, and I won't do anything right away. I guess I'll talk to Brian about this. He helps me see straight, sometimes."

Lou said, "Hey, I'm going to the library, but I'll meet you after, and we can go to your place and work on the science project. Okay?"

"Cool! See you," Seth said, going inside Brian's office.

After a few minutes of general talk, Brian looked closely at Seth. "What's on your mind? You look like a man with a problem."

Seth was often startled at the way in which the therapist could sense something was wrong, even when he hadn't said anything much. During their first sessions, he might not have opened up about his feelings. But now, he started talking about what had been happening between him and his coach, and how unfair he felt it was.

"I could understand if I was being a jerk, or I couldn't do stuff right," he said, "But I may be the best player on the team, right now. I mean, I still have trouble dribbling, but otherwise, I'm doing great! He never lets up on me, never tells me I did a good job. At least Danny and Con sometimes say I did well, but not Wes."

"Danny and Con — the assistant coaches?" Brian asked.

Seth nodded. "I like them, and they like me . . . or I *thought* they did, anyway. Now, I don't know anymore."

Brian leaned back in his chair. "So, you figure that the coach has something against you. And you don't know what it is. That right?"

"Yeah. I even asked him what the problem was, but he tried to tell me there *was* no problem. But there *has* to be!"

"You're sure about that? That Wes doesn't like you?"

"What else could it be?" Seth asked.

Brian ran his hands through his hair. "Do you get along with the rest of the team? You like them, and they like you?"

"Sure! One guy, Pete Gould, he's a good friend now. And I get along with everyone else, too, including Danny and Con."

"And you're doing well as a player? No problems there?"

Seth felt annoyed. He had wanted a little sympathy, and all he was getting was questions. "It's like I said, except for dribbling, I'm doing everything well. Passing, shooting, defense — I'm quicker than anybody else, except Pete. I can maneuver the chair better, too."

Brian nodded. "Okay. Let's take it that you're the number-one player on . . . What's the name of the team?"

"We haven't picked a name yet," replied Seth. "We will, before our first game."

"You're the top player on the team, then. So, Wes is always giving you grief because he is some kind of bad guy and has just decided that you're the one he wants to pick on. Or . . ."

He stopped and looked at Seth, eyebrows raised.

After a minute, Seth couldn't stand it. "Or *what?*"

The therapist shrugged. "You tell me. Isn't there anything you can think of to explain what's happening here? I mean, you tell me that Danny and Con are your buddies, and they don't have a problem with what the coach is doing. Maybe something's going on here that you haven't worked out yet."

Seth fought back a temptation to shout that he knew *exactly* what was going on, and took a deep breath. Working with Brian had taught him that it never solved anything to get mad and yell. Instead, he thought hard.

"Maybe . . . maybe he thinks I should be doing better. Even though I'm doing pretty well, maybe he wants me to do better. Except . . . *why?* If I'm doing well already?"

"You're doing so well that you couldn't possibly be doing better?" Brian smiled at Seth. "Is that what you mean?"

Seth snorted. "Of course not! You can always do better! But if he said something nice once in a while, I might want to work even harder. Why not give me a break sometimes?"

Brian sighed. "I can't tell you the answer to that one. Everybody has his own way of working, and there are probably reasons why this coach does what he does. You might want to keep thinking about what they could be."

Seth nodded. "I guess."

"You still thinking about quitting the team?"

"I guess not right now, anyway. I'll stick it out a little longer."

Brian grinned at Seth. "I think you made a good decision. See? That's *my* way of working, to let you know when you do something good."

✿   ✿   ✿

68

Later that afternoon, Seth and Lou were in Seth's room, working together on their science project, when Phyllis knocked on the door and stuck her head in. "How was practice?"

Seth made a face. "Okay, I guess."

"Is there a problem?" she asked.

Seth explained what was going on between him and the coach. Lou said, "Seth thinks that the coach has a grudge against him, but I'm not so sure."

Phyllis came into the room and leaned against the door. "You remember how I used to complain about my math teacher in seventh grade? How she was always giving me a hard time, and I thought she was totally unfair?"

"Yeah, I remember," said Seth. "But you changed your mind later on, right?"

"Right. I found out she had decided I was really good at math and that I could goof off all year and still get a good grade. But she knew I could do better than good, so she made sure I wouldn't loaf. And now I feel grateful to her."

Lou sat up. "Maybe that's it! Maybe the coach thinks you're so good he wants you to make the most of your talent."

Seth shrugged, but the idea stayed with him and was still in his head when he went to sleep that night.

Could it be that Wes had especially high expectations for him? And, if so, was it worth putting up with a lot of grief to try to meet those expectations?

9

"Listen up, guys!" Wes had just assembled the team to begin practice. "I have a few things to say before we go to work. First off, we'll be playing our first game one week from tonight, a team from the next county."

Seth and Pete grinned at each other and a few players began to talk excitedly among themselves. Wes raised a hand and everybody fell silent. "This other team, the Tigers, has been together for a year already. Some of them are pretty experienced, so we have our work cut out for us to get ready. Today, you're going to play some three-on-three.

"One other thing: This team doesn't have a name yet. I was thinking we could call ourselves the Wizards — well, the *Junior* Wizards — after the team that Danny and Con play for. I like the name, and

71

we can use some of their old jerseys. Would that be all right?"

Nobody had a problem with the name.

"Okay, enough talk. Let's warm up, and then we'll play."

As part of the warmups, Wes ran another relay race, the kind that had messed Seth up several days before. Now, Seth had no problem at all. In fact, he was among the faster dribblers on the team. Only Pete could beat him up and down the court. Wes said nothing to Seth, which, Seth now knew, was a good sign.

Generally, Seth had improved. He had developed calluses on his hands so that they no longer got rubbed raw when he used them as brakes to bring the chair to a quick stop. His shooting range had improved; he could hit from farther outside with fair accuracy, although he wasn't ready to try three-pointers yet. He could make hard chest passes and bounce passes, and was becoming a deft ball-handler.

And his arms and upper body were a *lot* stronger, too.

After the warmups, Wes put together two teams of three players each: two of the Junior Wizards would team up with either Danny or Con. Wes watched closely from the sidelines, made frequent criticisms, and rotated new players into the lineups.

Seth started off teamed with Con and a guy named James Jacks, a whip-thin boy who wore heavy leg braces that allowed him to walk, although slowly. As play began, Seth took an inbounds pass from James and wheeled downcourt, with Danny trying to hem him in and slow him down. Spotting Con making a break toward the basket, Seth threw a long bounce pass that Con scooped up without slowing down. Pete, one of the opponents, tried to catch him, but Con was too fast and laid the ball in a moment later.

"Pete!" yelled Wes from the sideline. "You falling asleep out there? Keep your eye on your man!" Pete flushed, but said nothing.

Seth began to realize that it wasn't easy keeping an eye on his man *and* watching to see where the ball was, too. Sure enough, a minute later, as he guarded Danny, Pete whizzed past him on the baseline, caught a pass, and put a short shot in off the glass.

"Watch the lanes, Seth!" came Wes's voice. "Keep your head on a swivel! You should have seen that one coming! Stay awake out there, everybody!"

Pete caught Seth's eye and Seth smiled and shrugged. He was getting used to Wes's style of coaching, and the criticism didn't sting as much as it had. And Danny had been right about Wes: He almost never praised anyone.

Seth ran down a rebound after Danny missed a long shot, and looked for a target for an outlet pass. Con tried to pivot his chair sharply, but James's chair caught Con's while Con was leaning the wrong way, and Con spilled out of the chair onto the hardwood. Wes whistled the play dead, and Seth sped over to help Con up.

As he came over, Con saw him and waved him away, looking angry. Seth backed off.

"Remember, don't help anyone who falls unless he asks you for help," whispered Danny from just behind Seth's shoulder. Meanwhile, Con had levered himself back into his chair and was ready to go again.

A moment later, Wes sent another Wizard in for Seth, who went to the sideline and thought about Con's reaction when Seth had instinctively come to help. He recalled when he had fallen and Wes had insisted he get into his chair unassisted.

You all need to be as independent as possible, Wes

had said. It was hard to argue with that. Danny and Con were good examples. He wanted to be as independent as possible, too.

Out of the corner of his eye, he saw that Lou had come into the gym and was leaning against a wall, watching. When his eye met Seth's, he waved. Seth nodded in return and shifted his attention back to the game.

As he did, the coach said, "That's right, Pender, keep your eyes on the court. This is what you're here for, remember?"

Just then, Pete let a pass from Danny get by him and roll out of bounds. "Good hands, Pete!" the coach called, sarcastically. "Maybe we can tape a couple of handles on the ball for you. Why don't you come out for a minute and think about what you did wrong just then? Seth, go in for him."

Pete looked unhappy as he passed Seth on his way into the game. Seth gave the other boy a wink and took his place on the court.

Seth, Danny, and James were now on defense. Danny whispered to try a zone, with himself under the basket and the other boys on either side and in front of him.

Con dribbled forward and stopped a few feet behind the key. When a defender came toward him, Con whipped a pass out to a teammate in the corner, who started in toward the basket. But Seth had anticipated the move and raced forward to block the other player, who rammed his chair into Seth's, hard.

Wes's whistle stopped the play. "Seth was in position. That's a charge on the offense. Danny's team, inbound the ball."

Danny took an inbounds pass from Seth, passed to James, then raced downcourt. James pivoted and passed to Seth, who dribbled fast and furious downcourt until a defender wheeled in front of him. He paused, keeping his dribble, and thought about shooting. But he was too far out. He faked with his head, and the defender moved ever so slightly with the fake. That was all Seth needed. He dribbled closer, dropped a bounce pass to Danny behind him, and set his chair in a perfect pick. With Seth keeping defenders away, Danny lofted a shot that hit nothing but net.

"*Yes!*" Danny shouted, and Wes whistled to end the game.

"Good shot, Danny," he said. Turning to the Junior Wizards, he shook his head. "You guys still have a lot of work to do. Tomorrow, we'll work on a few of the biggest problems, and play some more three-on-three. I want to see more concentration on the court tomorrow! Keep your eye on the ball! Anticipate on defense! Remember that you're a team! Okay, that's it for today."

Lou came up to Seth and Pete as they headed off the court. "You guys looked all right out there. Seth, that was a great pick you set."

Pete looked around to make sure that the coach was nowhere nearby, but Wes was talking to Con and paying them no attention. "You'd never know we ever did anything right if you listened to the coach," he said, scowling. "He never lets up, never eases off."

The three boys left the gym and headed for the parking lot, where Mrs. Pender would pick them up. "I felt the same way you do," Seth said to Pete, "but now I've changed my mind. I think he knows what he's doing."

Lou laughed. "I can't believe my ears! After the way you were putting him down last week. What happened between then and now?"

Seth smiled. "I just see things a little differently, that's all."

"Well, I don't!" Pete's expression was stony. "I still think he's just a bully who gets off on bossing us around."

"Well, I think he's teaching us a lot, and not just about basketball," Seth replied. "Like he said, we have to learn to be independent, and he wants us to toughen up. That's why he is the way he is, I think."

Pete looked surprised. "You're defending him? Well, I don't agree with you. Anyway, I better go. See you tomorrow."

As he left, Lou asked, "Is he mad at you?"

"I hope not," Seth said. He saw Danny just behind them and nodded.

"That was a really good pick you set," Danny said. "Also, I heard what Pete and you were saying. Don't worry, Pete isn't in any trouble. But I have to tell you, you sure have come a long way. You'd never have talked like that when I first met you. You're doing great!"

He raised a hand, and he and Seth exchanged high fives. It was a moment Seth would remember for a long time.

10

Seth looked at himself in the locker-room mirror, admiring the black jersey with *WIZARDS* across the front in gold letters, with gold lightning bolts running down the sides. Pete came up alongside him and smiled.

"Lookin' *good!*" he said, adjusting his own jersey. The Junior Wizards' jerseys had belonged to Danny and Con's older Wizard team. Seth and his teammates were about to play their first game, at the school where several of their opponents were students.

Danny came up and asked, "How are you guys feeling? You up for this?"

"Absolutely!" Seth replied, hoping his voice didn't sound as nervous as he felt.

"We're *ready!*" Pete added.

"Remember," Danny cautioned, "this team has been playing awhile and they're well-coached. We played against one of the Tiger coaches last year. Just remember what you've learned and stay cool."

Seth's throat felt dry, and he licked his lips. If they could give this team a game and not get blown out, that would be fine with him. His family and Lou were out there, and he didn't want to be embarrassed.

From the locker-room door, Wes called out, "I'd like the team on the court in a minute, so we can go over a few things. Con, Danny, come with me."

Danny clenched a fist and raised it over his head. "All right! Play tough and take no prisoners! See you outside."

As he came out of the locker room, Seth looked down to the end of the court, where the Tigers were warming up. They were doing the same drills that Seth and the Wizards did, but, somehow they looked *better,* as if this was stuff they had worked on for a long time, not just a few weeks. The Tigers looked assured, and they talked it up during the warmups. They had ten players to the Wizards' eight.

A handful of Wizard supporters clapped and cheered as they hit the floor; Danny spotted his family and Lou, and Lou flashed him a thumbs-up sign. There were more Tiger rooters, however, a few with signs and banners. Pete wheeled himself next to Seth. "They look tough," he whispered. "Look at the guy with the black headband! He just hit a twenty-footer!"

Wes clapped his hands sharply, and the Wizards huddled around him. Seth thought that Wes looked nervous, which made him feel even more uptight.

"Listen up!" snapped Wes. "We've worked hard, so let's make that work pay off. I know there have been times when you've been hating my guts. . . . Probably most of you do right now."

Several players laughed, and Seth suddenly felt a little better.

"The team you'll be playing against today has a full year of experience. Only four of them are as new to this game as all of you are. The Tiger coach emphasizes defense. They'll switch from zone D to man-to-man and back again; try to recognize which they're using. They play aggressively, so keep your cool.

"If they're using a zone, try to flood the zone — move a few guys into one area so they have to scramble. When they play man defense, look to set picks and switches.

"When they have the ball, I'll signal what defense you should use. Move the ball on offense, keep your passes sharp, and *talk* to each other, on offense and defense. Help each other out wherever you can. Keep your heads on swivels, keep your eyes on the ball, and give it a hundred percent. If you play your best, then you're doing a good job, win or lose. And, win or lose, this game will be a valuable learning experience for you all.

"Let's have your hands." All the Wizards stuck their hands into the middle of the huddle, and Wes covered their hands with his. "Are you ready?"

"*YEAH!*" they shouted.

Wes named the starters, including Seth and Pete, and assured everyone that they'd get plenty of playing time. "You'll get breathers, and you'll need them, I promise you."

"You bet you will," echoed Con, with a smile.

"Remember what you've been working on," Danny urged, as the teams took the court. The two referees had the team members shake hands. One ref tossed a coin to see who would get the ball, and Pete called, "Tails."

The coin came up tails, and Pete inbounded the ball from under the Wizards' basket. He threw a bounce pass to Seth, who headed toward midcourt, dribbling and checking to see what defense the Tigers were using. Suddenly, a hand reached in and whipped the ball away. A Tiger had come up on Seth's blind side for the steal. Two Wizards were racing downcourt, unaware of the turnover.

"Hey!" Pete yelled, moving toward the man with the ball, who flipped it to a teammate waiting under the Wizards' basket. The man put in the easy shot, and the Tigers led, 2–0.

"Watch the ball!" bellowed Wes.

The Wizards brought the ball upcourt again, and Seth saw Pete unguarded twelve feet from the basket. As he fired a pass, two Tigers converged on Pete and had him trapped in the corner. Pete searched desperately for someone to pass to, and James Jacks wheeled toward him, waving an arm. Pete hurled a baseball-style pass in James's direction, but James couldn't control the ball, which rolled out of bounds.

The ref whistled the ball dead, and the Tigers put it in play.

Seth glanced at his family and Lou in the stands as he raced back on defense. A Tiger player with awesome biceps sped past Seth, and he tried to catch up. Looking back over his shoulder, he saw a pass headed toward the Tiger, who was intent on an easy fast-break basket. He gave his wheels a hard pump and lunged forward, reaching out a hand and deflecting the ball out of bounds, foiling the easy basket. On the sideline, the other Wizard players clapped.

"Good D!" called Con. As the Tigers put the ball in play, a muscular Tiger forced his way next to the key, just to the side of the basket. When a teammate's shot went off the rim, he tipped the ball out to another Tiger. Seth tried to muscle him away from his spot, but the guy was too big and strong. The Tiger rebounded another shot and bounced the ball to a player on the baseline, who sank it despite being rammed by Pete. The ref called Pete for a foul, and the Tiger hit the free throw. It was 5–0. Wes signaled for a time-out.

Seth felt stunned as the Wizards huddled around

their coaches. "Welcome to the world of wheelchair basketball," said Con.

Pete scowled and muttered, "These guys are too much for us."

Seth snapped, "What are you talking about? We're going to get better!" He suddenly felt a competitive anger he hadn't felt since before his accident.

"Quiet, everybody!" Wes said. "We've only played a couple of minutes, so don't panic. I called time so you wouldn't lose your heads out there. Remember, these guys are veterans, and this is your first time. Remember your prepared plays and stick to them. We'll play a half-court game for now, no fast breaks, just move the ball around and be alert.

"Always know where your opponents are and where the ball is. On that first play, some of you rushed downcourt without bothering to make sure the ball was coming with you. *Keep an eye on the ball!* Otherwise, you're in for hard times. Now, take your time, look for good shots. Remember your basic plays: pick-and-roll, give-and-go, all that stuff. When you have the ball, find an open man. When you don't have the ball, *get* open.

85

"All right! Let's show this team that they can't just roll over us!"

Seth took the inbound pass, tossed to James, and got the ball back at midcourt. Sensing movement on his left, he yanked the ball away just before a Tiger defender could snatch it. The Tigers were in a tight man-to-man defense. Suddenly, Pete made a quick pivot, and Seth whipped him the ball. Pete lofted a twelve-footer that went in off the glass to make the score 5–2.

During the next few minutes, Seth and his teammates realized that the Tigers, while more experienced, weren't supermen. At one point, James made a steal and Seth converted a fast-break layup. Seth's arms were aching, though, when Wes sent in subs for him and Pete with three minutes left in the first quarter.

Con came over as Seth caught his breath. "Good move on the fast break!"

Seth wiped his face with a towel. "We *can* play with these guys! *Way to go, James!*"

The wiry James had just drawn a charging foul by getting into the lane and holding his position against a Tiger who was trying a layup. When the Wizards scored on a slick give-and-go, the score was 9–6; the Wizards were only three down.

At the end of the quarter, however, the Tigers led, 11–6. During the second quarter, Seth was all over the court. He made steals, assists, and an outstanding defensive play when he lunged to knock a Tiger pass out of bounds and fell out of his chair in the process. He waved away offers of assistance and got back in the chair, while even Tiger fans applauded. Pete made some great moves with his chair and shook loose for a few shots. As a team, the Wizards showed that they, too, could play tough defense. At halftime, the Tiger lead was only 22–20.

Wes didn't actually smile during halftime, but he admitted that the team had had some good moments. When he said this, Seth winked at Pete, who grinned.

"In the second half," said Wes, "let's try a full-court press on them, see if that rattles their brains. Also, if you see a fast-break chance, go for it. We might catch them by surprise. And keep up the D — no easy baskets." He looked around. "Danny, Con? Anything to add?"

Con said, "Their guy in the black headband loves

shooting from downtown. Give him room and let him bomb away — he's not as good as he thinks he is."

"All right!" Wes leaned forward. "This is your game to win! Go out and fight!"

Early in the third quarter, the Wizard full-court press created two turnovers that led to easy baskets, and the Wizards were in the lead, 24–22! The teams exchanged baskets for a few minutes before the Tiger coach called time to make adjustments. Later in the quarter, the Tigers took the lead back, and the period ended with the Wizards down, 32–28.

Looking around between quarters, Seth realized that the Wizards were tired; the extra Tiger players kept them fresher.

With the Wizards down by four at the start of the fourth quarter, Wes sent Seth and James back into the game. Seth felt rested and sank a shot off a beautiful pass from Pete, cutting the Tiger lead to two.

But that was as close as the Wizards could get. The Tigers tired the Wizards out, and, even though there were no serious defensive goofs, the Tigers pulled away to win, 43–34.

Afterward, several Tiger players came over and

congratulated Seth on his play. One said, "I figured this game would be a laugher, but I was wrong."

Seth's family came up and praised his play. Phyllis hugged her brother. "I am *so proud* of you!"

Lou nodded, smiling. "You guys are going to win some games, I *know* it!"

Wes called the team together. "As far as I'm concerned," he said, "this was a *win*. You did a great job, and you're going to get better. We'll work more on conditioning, so you don't run out of gas late in the games."

While Mr. Pender drove the Penders and Lou for some ice cream, Lou asked Seth, "Are you down about losing the game?"

Seth thought for a second and grinned. "No way! This is only the beginning! You wait and see!"

11

I don't know," Lou said, as he and Seth left school on a sunny afternoon. "Can *you* understand what we were taught in math today? *I* don't get it, that's for sure."

Seth grinned. "I think I'm going to ask Phyllis for a little help tonight. She's the math whiz. Come over if you want."

"Hey, thanks. Maybe she can tell me what *x* is and why it keeps changing all the time." Lou scratched his head. "It was so much easier in eighth grade." Seth and Lou had both turned fourteen the previous month.

They were at an intersection, waiting for a green light, when a car pulled up near them and Danny Detweiler stuck his head out of the driver's-side window.

"Yo, Seth! Hey Lou! I *thought* it was you two I saw!"

Seth was delighted to see Danny, whom he hadn't heard from in several months. The Junior Wizard team on which he'd played had wound up having a decent season, winning three games and losing three. Seth had improved with each game, ending up with an eight-point-per-game scoring average. His friend Pete Gould had led the team in assists, and Pete had stayed friendly with Seth and Lou through summer vacation, spending time with them and their friends.

"How are you doing?" asked Seth. "Hey, cool car, by the way!"

Danny grinned. "I just got it last week! It's got hand controls for the gas and brakes. I have some big news!"

"What's up?" Lou asked.

Danny held up a letter and waved it toward them. "I just heard I've won a college scholarship! I'll be going in the fall. This college has a fantastic wheelchair athletic program, one of the best in the country!"

"All *right!*" Seth yelled, stretching out a hand and pumping Danny's.

"That's really great!" added Lou. "Will you be playing basketball there?"

"Absolutely!" Danny nodded happily. "I have to really train, starting now. They're always among the top-rated teams nationwide. And I'm aiming at the Paralympics a few years down the road."

Seth felt happy for his friend, but he had to admit that he also felt sad that Danny would be headed elsewhere soon — out of his life, for the most part. He hoped his dismay didn't show.

"The other news is for Seth," Danny went on. "You'll be getting a call in the next few days from a guy named Howard Sturgis. He's the coach of my old team — you know, the *real* Wizards. They want you to come to practice when they start up."

Lou turned to Seth and slapped him on the back. "Hey, *fantastic!* You'll make it, too!"

"That's what Wes and I told Howard," said Danny, looking closely at Seth. "You look like you're not so sure. What's the problem? I figured you'd be happy about this."

"Huh? Oh, *sure* I'm happy," Seth said. "I . . . What about Pete? Could he come, too?"

Danny nodded. "We recommended him. Both of you guys can help that team. Seth? You don't look like a man who just heard a piece of very good news. How come?"

Seth shook his head. "No, no, I know it's good. Really. I guess I just hope I don't let you down, that's all. Plus, I'm going to miss you when you go away."

Danny looked up at Lou, and back to Seth. "Well, first of all, I don't think for a second that you'll let me down. I know you sometimes aren't sure of what you can do, but *I* know, and so does my man, Lou here. Right?"

"Absolutely," Lou replied. "Seth can do whatever he has a mind to."

"And Wes knows, too," Danny went on. "He had you spotted as a comer from day one, last year. Why do you think he gave you such a hard time? He didn't want you to sell yourself short, was all. And you didn't.

"As for me going away, that isn't going to be until the fall. I'll be around for months, playing ball with another team. I'll be checking out your practices and seeing your games, too. You're not getting rid of me yet."

"You can sit with us, in our rooting section," said Lou. "I plan on seeing every Wizards game, me and our buddies. We know that Seth is going to do the job."

Danny smiled at Lou, but his expression turned more serious as his eyes met Seth's. "Understand, you're going to have to work hard with these new guys. Just the way you did last year. It's a new challenge. But you can meet it. Just remember, the toughest tests are the ones you want to pass the most. That's the way it ought to be. That's what life is all about: taking on challenges and meeting them. Right?"

Seth stared into Danny's eyes and nodded. "Right."

"Okay!" Danny looked at his watch. "I have to get going. Listen, I'll be seeing you soon. You all right with this?"

"Fine," Seth answered. "And that's great about the scholarship."

Danny smiled. "Lou, save a seat for me in the rooting section. Take it easy, guys."

As he drove away, Lou turned back to Seth. "You *are* all right with it, aren't you? Danny's right. You're ready. You'll make the team."

"Yeah, I . . . I will. I *will*." Seth turned his chair toward the intersection. "We'd better get moving."

"Okay." As they crossed the street, Lou sighed.

"What's the matter?" asked Seth.

"I just hope Phyllis can help me with this math stuff," Lou muttered. "But I have my doubts."

"Sure she will," Seth said, grinning. "Hey, look at it like a new challenge. The toughest tests are the ones most worth passing. Right?"

"Right!" said Lou, and both boys laughed.

"Tomorrow's the day I have my first workout with the Wizards," said Seth, whose eyes remained fixed on the carpet as his fingers tapped restlessly on the arms of his chair. "Howard, the coach, called over the weekend. That's the major news."

Brian Murtaugh smiled at the boy. "I'd say it's pretty big! Exciting, too, I think. But never mind how *I* feel about it, how do *you* feel?"

"Me?" Seth looked up at the therapist. "How *should* I feel? I feel great!"

Brian's eyebrows raised in a look of surprise. "Really? Great, huh? That's why you're doing a drum routine with your fingers on your chair, to show how great you feel?"

Startled, Seth pulled his hands into his lap. "I didn't even know I was doing that. But I really do feel great. My family think's it's great, Danny thinks it's great, my best friend, Lou, thinks it's great, so how else should I feel?"

Brian leaned back and laced his fingers behind his head. "Let's forget about how you *should* feel for the moment, and think about how you *really* feel. And don't say 'great' again, okay? Don't try to con Uncle Brian, we know each other too well."

Seth felt his face go red and was angry for just a second, but then laughed. "Okay, Uncle Brian, I guess you're too sharp for me."

"That's why *I'm* the doctor and *you're* the patient. I agree that this ought to make you feel very good; it's a big step up in a sport that is very important to you. The question is: How come you don't actually feel that way?"

"Well . . ." Seth closed his eyes and said nothing for a minute. Then he looked at Brian. "What if I'm not ready? What if I'm not good enough to cut it? These guys are older, they're better. What if they say, 'Come back next year,' or even, 'Don't come back at all?'"

Brian nodded slowly. "It could happen, I suppose. Danny and Wes might be wrong about you. These guys think you have what it takes, but maybe they're both off the mark. What would happen then?"

"I don't know!" Seth took a breath. "It'd be bad. I'd feel like a . . . like a total loser."

"Another thing, Wes and Danny and Con really helped me and encouraged me and made sure I did the right things and believed in myself. They won't be around now. Con is going to college, like Danny. Without them, I don't know. I might turn out to be a . . ."

"A loser?" Brian asked, softly.

Seth just stared at him.

"Let's think back a couple of years," suggested Brian. "Think about when you first started seeing me. Remember how you were then, the way you thought and felt?"

"Yeah. I was angry a lot of the time. . . ."

"*All* the time . . . ," Brian corrected.

Seth smiled. "I felt sorry for myself and didn't want to have anything to do with anyone. I thought my life was over."

"That's a good summary." Brian leaned toward Seth. "When you think about yourself then and now, how far you've come, the progress you've made physically, mentally, emotionally, can you really see yourself as a *loser?* Could a *loser* have done all that?"

Seth smiled. "Well, no, but —"

Brian held up a hand like a policeman stopping traffic. "No but! *No . . . but!* You are not a loser. You are a *winner* and a *doer.*

"You've found out a lot about yourself during the last couple of years, things you might not have learned so soon if you hadn't had that accident. But you still don't know how strong you are. I think you'll be surprised to discover that there's more to you than you know of yet.

"More strength, and I don't just mean muscles, either. Here's what I know: You'll go there tomorrow and you'll give it your best shot. Here's what I believe: You'll do just fine. And you'll put some of your doubts to rest."

Seth thought about it. Then he said, "Will you come to any games?"

Brian nodded. "I'll be there."

13

How does that new chair feel?" asked Mrs. Pender, who was dropping Seth off at the school where the Wizards were practicing.

"Unbelievable!" said Seth, moving it around, testing its maneuverability. "It's so *light!*" The Penders had gotten Seth the chair with the aid of a foundation that helped pay for expensive chairs for wheelchair athletes. The frame was made of a superlight alloy that was also used on the finest racing bicycles. Seth *felt* like a better player in it.

"Seth!" Pete Gould came toward him from the door of the school. "How's —"

Seeing the new chair, he stopped short, and his eyes widened. "*Wow*," he whispered. "That is an *awesome* set of wheels!"

Seth smiled. "We got it last night. There's this organization that gave us part of what it cost. I'll tell you how to find them."

Pete stared at the chair. "That'd be great." Finally he tore his eyes away and looked at Seth. "You ready for this?"

Seth licked his lips. "Yeah, I guess. . . . I mean, *sure!* You?"

Pete laughed nervously. "As ready as *you* are. I mean, Wes and Danny say we are."

"Right!" Seth took a deep breath. "So, let's go."

In the gym, half a dozen Wizards were scattered around the floor, shooting balls or working on their chairs. At first nobody seemed to notice the new-comers. Seth started out on the floor, and Pete followed.

"They don't like us," he whispered.

"Be cool," Seth whispered back. "They haven't known you long enough to dislike you."

"Very funny," Pete muttered.

A dark-haired boy in a sleeveless sweatshirt turned to them. "How you doing? Are you Seth and Pete? I'm Gil Marin."

Seth and Pete introduced themselves, and a few others came forward to give their names. One of them, a thin blond named Andy with muscular fore-arms and huge hands, gestured toward Seth's chair.

"Great chair. That a Tornado?"

Seth nodded. "Yeah, it's brand-new."

"Ernie has a Tornado," said Gil, looking around. "Guess he's not here yet. You guys want to get warm, grab a ball and shoot."

"Thanks," Pete said, scooping up a loose ball and moving closer to a basket. Seth did the same, and lofted a twelve-footer than banged off the rim.

As he put up a few shots, Seth began to relax, feel-ing comfortable in a familiar routine. A few other players arrived, including Ernie, whose chair was like Seth's, except that his wheels were angled more. There wasn't much chatter; everyone concentrated on their warmup.

As Seth sank a fifteen-foot shot off the board, Ernie came up. "You like that chair?"

Ernie looked to be sixteen and wore a baseball cap with the bill turned backward.

"Yeah!" replied Seth. "You like yours?"

"Uh-huh." Ernie pointed down to the front wheels. "I adjusted the camber because I get more control when I — we'll talk later. Here come the coaches."

Two men had arrived, one in a wheelchair, the other, walking. The one in the chair stuck two fingers in his mouth and gave a piercing whistle. The boys gathered around.

"Everyone here?" asked the man who had whistled. He looked around and saw Seth and Pete. "I'm Howard Sturgis, and this is our other coach, Chan McGuire. Which of you is Seth and which is Pete?"

The boys introduced themselves, and Howard saw that they had met the rest of the team.

"We have a lot to do, so let's get to it," said Chan. "For the benefit of the new guys — and anyone who needs reminding — we don't have stars here. We're a *team,* period. We don't do much warmup; you're expected to keep yourselves in shape.

"What we do, mostly, in practice is learn offensive and defensive sets and plays and *drill* them. It'll be hard, especially at first, and you may find it dull. But you'll find that it will all pay off when we play. Any questions? Good."

The Wizards split into squads and ran plays. They

didn't work on things like dribbling; you were supposed to know how. Seth couldn't remember ever working as hard.

Each coach ran a squad, and they worked on weaves, single and double picks and screens, and other offenses, running them over and over as the coaches pointed out errors in positioning or mechanics, repeating each play until Seth ached and thought he might faint.

Finally, just as Seth was ready to beg for a breather, Howard whistled. Seth was relived to see that the other players were also breathing hard and sweating. It wasn't just him.

"Everyone, take ten," Howard called out. "Then we'll run five-on-five plays and work defensive sets."

Pete groaned softly. "You mean we're not done? There's more? *Arrrggghhh!*"

Ernie grinned at Pete. "You ready to hang it up? We're just getting started!"

Pete rolled his eyes and said, "If I don't make it, tell my folks I loved 'em."

Gil and Ernie laughed.

When practice resumed, the coaches went over

defensive sets the team would use: two-three, three-two, and diamond-and-one zones, and full- and half-court presses. The team split into squads to work defenses and demonstrate ways to beat them on offense.

Seth's arms and upper body began to ache again, but he was still finding the session fascinating and learning a lot.

Shortly before practice ended, Seth's squad tried a formation designed to break a full-court press. He raced to midcourt, where he fielded a baseball-style pass from Ernie. Turning downcourt, he saw Andy wheeling hard for the baseline and fired a long bounce pass. Andy caught it without slowing down and flipped in a layup. He turned to Seth and gave him a clenched-fist salute. Seth suddenly felt wonderful and forgot about the fatigue he had been feeling just seconds ago.

He turned and spotted Danny sitting at courtside. The older boy nodded.

"All right!" called Chan. "That's it for now. Get your rest and be set to go tomorrow!"

Danny called, "Good assist, there."

"Thanks," Seth said. "That was rough!"

"Sure," Danny agreed. "But you and Pete are fitting right in."

Seth was startled. "Really? Nobody said a word to us."

Danny laughed. "Of course not! Don't you get it by now?"

Seth thought for a moment. "I guess nobody wastes much time being nice, do they?"

"In this sport," Danny said, "when someone gives you a compliment, it's something really special."

Seth thought back to the clenched fist Andy had flashed a minute ago. "Yeah, I see that it is."

Seth winced at the shrill sound of Howard's two-finger whistle. The coach was standing next to him with a scowl on his face, an expression the Wizards dreaded.

"Come on, Ernie, get your brain in gear!" the coach snapped. "You should've handled that pass! It was right in your hands!"

"Sorry, I blew it," mumbled Ernie, looking apologetic. "No excuse."

"You *bet* there's no excuse!" Howard growled. "I guarantee you, pull that tomorrow and the Lobos will make you pay for it."

The next night, the Lobos would be the Wizards' first opponents of the season. Howard had a quick, whispered conversation with Chan, who clapped his hands sharply. "Let's take a break. Then we'll work on some plays that looked pretty shabby today. The starters will start on offense against the subs, and I don't want to see any silly mistakes when we get back to work!"

Seth and Pete, who were both substitutes, went for some water. Ernie joined them. "Coach can get rough when he wants to," said Pete.

Ernie shrugged. "No big deal. I've heard it all before. Anyway, he was *right,* no way I should let that pass get by me."

Andy, another starter, who had lost both legs just above the knee at the age of six, joined them. He studied Seth's chair and asked, "You like that cushion? It looks uncomfortable."

"No, it's fine," said Seth. "I tried one that I thought would be easier on my back, but this gives me better support."

"You guys know anything about the Lobos?" Pete asked.

"They were great last year," Ernie said. "But two of their key guys are gone, and I don't know how that'll affect them."

"We ought to play them tough," added Andy, "if

our bench doesn't let us down." He winked at Ernie, who snickered.

Seth grinned. "Don't worry, we'll bail you out when you get into trouble, right, Pete?"

Straight-faced, Pete nodded. "Definitely. Just call us the Emergency Rescue Squad — there when you starters break down."

The second half of practice was almost as competitive as a game. Seth, Pete, and the other substitutes played their hardest and gave the starters all they could handle. Playing man-to-man defense, Seth guarded Gil for several minutes and stuck to him stubbornly. Gil kept trying quick feints and spins in an effort to get open for a pass, but couldn't do it for several possessions in a row. Finally, he broke away by taking advantage of a pick set by Ernie, and sank a ten-foot shot.

But Seth darted forward to steal a pass almost out of Gil's hands a moment later and fired a long pass to Pete, who had broken toward the other end of the court. Pete, in turn, bounced a beautifully timed lead pass to a sub named Mick, who scored.

"What's going on here?" Howard called out.

"Maybe we got things backward. The subs are making you starters look like losers! Gil, you should have been able to screen Seth off that pass! Seth, Pete . . . heads up playing there!"

Seth and Pete were careful not to gloat, but they flashed each other a quick look of satisfaction. A few minutes later, the coaches ended the session. Gil edged over to Seth.

"You were making me sweat today! Glad you're on our side."

"I got lucky, that's all," replied Seth. "You've been burning me just about every time I try to guard you — up till today."

As the players headed to the locker room, Chan tapped Seth's shoulder. "Get a good night's sleep. I want to see you look as good in the game as you did today in practice."

The Wizards-Lobos game had drawn a fairly sizable crowd that had half-filled the bleachers in the gym. As he completed his warmups, Seth spotted his family and Lou and was happy to note that Danny was there, too, sitting just in front of them. A moment later, he saw that Brian Murtaugh had also come to see the game. It would be the first time the therapist had watched Seth play.

As the game began, it was clear to Seth that the Lobos weren't as disciplined as the Wizards; maybe losing key players had made a difference. Led by Ernie and Andy, the defense shut the Lobos down. They could not get a shot off on their first five possessions. If the Wizards had converted most of their chances, they might have put the game out of reach in the first quarter. As it was, Andy scored a couple of early buckets and Gil had a three-point play, while Ernie forced two Lobo offensive fouls and made two steals.

Finally, two Lobos got their shooting touch back, and they got into the game. With two minutes left in the quarter, and the Wizards up, 11–8, Howard sent Seth and Pete into the game.

The Lobos inbounded the ball at midcourt, and one of them tried to sneak under the basket unguarded. However, Mick stole the ball and Seth, reacting quickly, pivoted and headed downcourt. Looking back over his shoulder, he saw Mick pass to Pete. Pete fired the ball toward him. Pete's pass was slightly underthrown, and Seth had to slow down to control it. He waited for his teammates to catch up, dropped the ball off to Mick on a give-and-go, and caught Mick's return pass while driving the lane. Before he could get off the shot, a Lobo rammed his chair into him and was whistled for a two-shot foul.

Seth went to the line, took a deep breath, and shot the first free throw. It rattled around the rim . . . and dropped in! His second free throw hit nothing but the net. Racing back on defense, Seth saw his sister and Lou standing and yelling their approval. Danny, too, cheered and clapped.

The Lobos scored on their next possession, staying within three. They tried a full-court press when the Wizards took over, but Mick hurled a long pass to Pete, who found Seth in the corner. Using fast, accurate passes, the Wizards were able to get Pete open for a twelve-foot shot. Unfortunately, the ball banged hard off the rim, into the hands of a Lobo.

Seth sped back on defense, noting that Chan had signaled for a diamond-and-one zone. Seth raced to get to his assigned position on the baseline, just as an opponent tried to get free underneath the basket. Seeing him, Seth moved forward into the lane, stopping just before the Lobo slammed into him. The ref's whistle stopped play, and the Lobo was called for a charge, giving the ball back to the Wizards. On the sideline, Seth's teammates pumped fists in the air and yelled encouragement. The Wizard rooters added their cheers.

Seth was tired when he came out of the game, but happy with his play. There were five minutes left in the half, and the Wizards were leading, 26–20. Seth exchanged high fives with several teammates before turning to watch as play resumed.

At halftime, the Wizards still held a six-point edge, 29–23. In the locker room, Howard Sturgis cut off the excited chatter of his team with his two-finger whistle. "Let's not get cocky," he said. "We caught the Lobos by surprise at first, but, in case you didn't notice, they're still in this game. They're only six back, and they played us pretty even for most of the first half. We can't afford to let down now. Keep playing all-out, and I'll bring in fresh troops whenever you need to rest.

"In the second half, we should use more zone defenses; look for my signals, and we'll keep changing looks to keep them off-balance. When they use zones on us, we'll try to flood the zones; you know how to do that. Any questions? All right, let's go!"

Sure enough, the Lobos *were* still in the game; they scored two quick baskets at the beginning of the half to cut the Wizard lead to two. For a few minutes, the teams swapped points, and when Seth came in again, the Wizards led, 37–35. A minute later, he slapped the ball away from a Lobo to start a Wizard fast break. Pete scored off a pass from Ernie to make the lead four.

In the last minute of the quarter, with the 35-second shot clock winding down, Seth found himself with the ball, hemmed in by two Lobo defenders with arms outstretched. Unable to see a teammate to pass to, Seth heaved a desperate hook shot, and was amazed to see it drop through the net. When the buzzer sounded the end of the quarter, Pete edged over to him.

"Been working on that play for long?"

Seth laughed. "Yeah, late at night, in my basement. It's my secret weapon."

Seth came out of the game for the start of the last quarter and watched anxiously as the Lobos wore down the Wizard defense. With four minutes left, the Lobos tied the game at 44. Chan came to Seth on the sideline. "Go in for Andy. That red-haired guy of theirs has the hot hand right now. See if you can cool him off. Get right in his shadow."

Seth nodded and took the floor. He tried to stay between his man and the ball, but the redhead broke free for a shot. Seth reached to block it, but caught the Lobo's arm, sending him to the free-throw line. He made one of two, giving the Lobos their first lead, a single point.

The Wizards brought the ball downcourt. Seth and Mick set a screen. Ernie put up a high-arcing shot that dropped in for a one-point Wizard edge. The crowd noise in the gym grew so loud that the players couldn't hear themselves talk.

The Lobos seemed to be tiring and threw the ball away on a bad pass. Chan signaled his players to use up some clock, so they moved into a weave, passing the ball back and forth, hoping to tire the Lobos still more, as well as run the clock down. Finally, with four seconds on the 35-second clock, Pete found Ernie in the corner, and the blond netted it to make the lead three points for the Wizards.

A wild Lobo shot bounced off the backboard into Pete's hands, and he threw an outlet pass to Ernie. Again, the Wizards began to eat up the clock. As it ran down, Seth faked one way, pivoted to the other side, and took a bounce pass from Pete, and banked in a shot. The score was 50–45 in favor of the Wizards as the final buzzer sounded.

The next fifteen minutes were happy confusion for Seth. After the players shook hands and went to the sidelines, his family rushed to congratulate him. Lou pounded him on the back, and Phyllis gave him a victory hug. Danny grabbed his hands, beaming.

"You looked *great* out there."

Seth felt dazed and totally happy. "Thanks," he said to Danny. "For everything."

Brian Murtaugh worked his way over to Seth and leaned in. "Congratulations," he said, quietly. "See you soon."

"It's pizza time!" Chan shouted. "Let's celebrate, guys! My treat!"

Seth was definitely ready to celebrate. He felt that he had done much more than win a game.

Have you thought about plans for the future?" asked Brian as he and Seth sat in the therapist's office.

"I want to keep playing wheelchair sports," Seth said. "Basketball for sure, and maybe others, too. I talked to Con about racing one day, and I might want to give that a try. I want to see what else is available."

"Sounds good," replied Brian. "What about life outside of sports? You thinking about those things, too?"

Seth nodded. "Sure! I guess I want to go to college someday. I mean, I'm pretty sure I do. My grades are good, and I might even be able to get a scholarship, like Danny."

"To do what?" Brian held up a hand. "Don't

misunderstand. College is a worthwhile goal. You want to keep your options open, and the more education you have, the more choices you have as you get older. I'm curious to know whether you've thought about what you may do as an adult. Not that you have to make any final decisions right now, of course."

"Well . . ." Seth was quiet for a moment. "For sure, I want to stay in athletics, college sports, maybe the Paralympics. If I have the talent. If I don't, I'll still give it my best shot."

He looked at Brian. "I *do* have an idea about what I want. You might think it's ridiculous. . . ."

"Never," Brian said. "I have a hunch that no goal of yours will sound ridiculous."

"Well, I think I might like to work with kids. You know, kids like I was when I first saw you, who need someone they can . . . who can give them help, all the things you did for me.

"Maybe I could be a coach, or maybe a therapist. I don't know exactly what yet, but that's the kind of thing I have in mind."

Brian smiled. "That's about as far from ridiculous as you can get. It sounds like a wonderful idea. I'll be happy to talk to you about that sometime, if you like. But there's another issue we need to discuss right now."

"Really? What's that?" Seth asked.

Brian stood up. "How would you feel if I said that you don't need these sessions with me anymore?"

Seth blinked. "Really?"

"As much as I like your company, Seth, I don't think you need what I've been doing for you. You've come a long way. I'd be happy to keep in touch, especially if you ever want to pick my brains about therapy or education. But getting together as we've been doing, I don't think it will serve any useful purpose."

Seth stared at the therapist. "Wow! I . . . I didn't see that coming. I don't know. . . ."

"If you think about it," Brian pointed out, "you'll realize that the day was going to come, sooner or later. My goal was to help you get through a tough time in your life. I'm not claiming that life will be a day at the beach from now on. *Nobody's* life is. But you can handle what comes along without leaning on me. I wouldn't say this to you if I weren't certain."

"Okay," Seth said, after a pause. "Okay, then. But I really want to stay in touch, maybe call you sometimes."

"Absolutely," Brian said. "Actually, I'm hoping I may be able to call on *you* sometimes."

"What do you mean?"

"In my work, I meet a lot of young people who are like you were two years ago. It might do a few of them a lot of good to be able to meet you, hear about your experiences. Would you be up for that? It could help you, too, especially if you want to do my kind of work someday."

"Yeah," Seth said. "Sure, I'd like that."

"Okay, then," said Brian. "I'll be in touch." He reached out a hand. "Take care of yourself."

Seth shook Brian's hand.

"Yeah. I will. I believe I will."

Matt Christopher

Terrell Davis

John Elway

Julie Foudy

Wayne Gretzky

Ken Griffey Jr.

Mia Hamm

Grant Hill

Derek Jeter

Randy Johnson

Michael Jordan

Lisa Leslie

Tara Lipinski

Mark McGwire

Greg Maddux

Hakeem Olajuwon

Briana Scurry

Emmitt Smith

Sammy Sosa

Mo Vaughn

Tiger Woods

Steve Young

The #1
Sports Writer
for Kids

MATT CHRISTOPHER

Read them all!

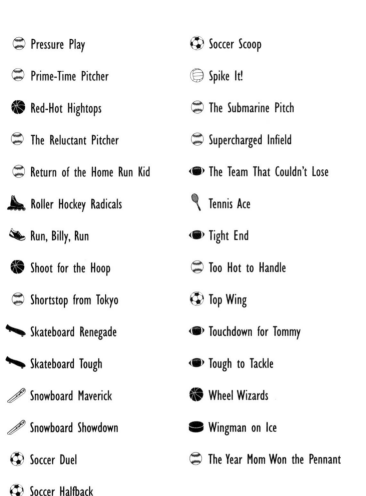
All available in paperback from Little, Brown and Company